Great SUPER BOWL Traditions

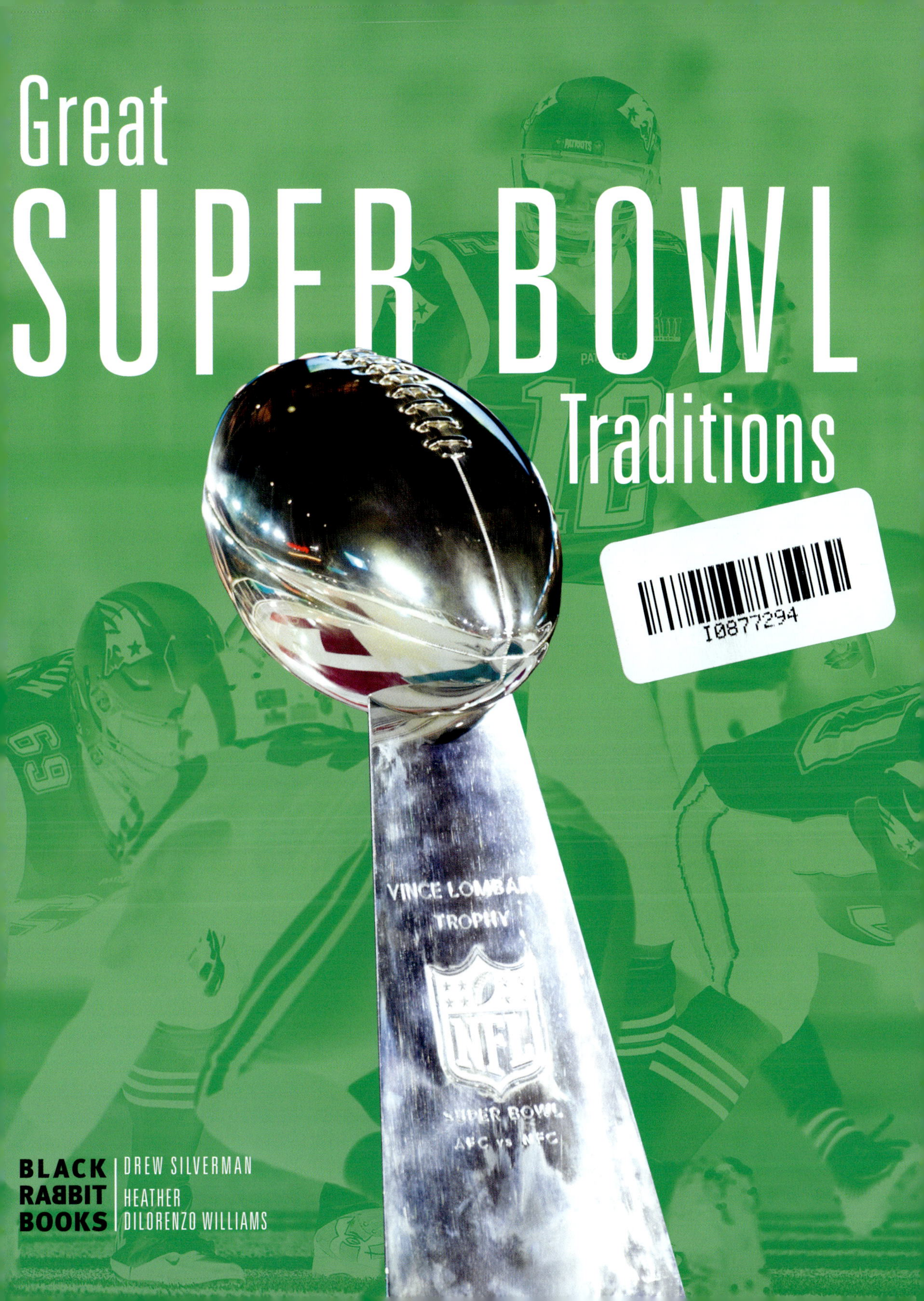

DREW SILVERMAN
HEATHER DILORENZO WILLIAMS

BLACK RABBIT BOOKS

TABLE OF CONTENTS

1 Super Bowl Greats

Good teams win the Super Bowl. Great teams win it again and again.

The Dallas Cowboys won the Super Bowl three times in four years. The San Francisco 49ers won four times in one decade. The Cowboys and the 49ers have won five Super Bowls each.

The Pittsburgh Steelers and the New England Patriots are Super Bowl greats. Each team has won six Super Bowls. The Steelers won four times between 1975 and 1980. The Patriots have won the big game six times since 2002.

Did You Know?

The Green Bay Packers won the first two Super Bowls. They have won two more times since then.

2

Must-Watch TV

Millions of people watch the Super Bowl every February. It is one of the biggest shows of the year. They tune in to see who the National Football League (NFL) champions will be. People like the halftime show too. They like watching new commercials during the game.

The 2024 Super Bowl was the most-watched Super Bowl of all time. More than 123 million people watched it. Some watched on television. Others watched on a computer. Some even watched on their phone. People could watch the big game anywhere.

Did You Know?
Every Super Bowl has been shown on live television.

3

Media Day

SUPER BO
25
GATORADE FROST

Teams show up a week early for the Super Bowl. Coaches and players meet with reporters. They talk to sports writers. Websites and TV stations ask them lots of questions. This is called **Media** Day.

Most of the questions are serious. Reporters talk about the game. They ask players how they are feeling. They ask coaches about their game plan.

But sometimes Media Day gets silly. Reporters might dress in funny outfits. Players join in too. They tell jokes or sing songs. Media Day is always a big event.

Think About It Pretend you are a sports reporter. What question would you ask your favorite athlete?

XLIX
ARIZONA
SUPER BOWL
XLIX
ARIZONA
SUPER BOW
GATORADE
SUPER BOWL
XLIX

4 Pregame

The Super Bowl starts in the evening. But many big moments happen before kickoff.

Fans like watching special shows about the Super Bowl. Sports experts talk about the game. They might even guess a winner.

Close to game time, famous singers perform. One sings "America the Beautiful." Another sings "The Star-Spangled Banner." Sometimes jets fly over the field.

At game time, an official flips a coin. A player calls "heads" or "tails." If the player guesses right, he decides which team gets the ball first. Now everyone is ready for the big game!

Did You Know?

The "heads" side of the Super Bowl coin is a picture of the Super Bowl trophy.

5

Don't Skip the Ads

The Super Bowl isn't just about football. Companies use the game to **advertise**. They know millions of people will see their commercials. They pay a lot of money for a Super Bowl ad. A 30-second commercial cost $7 million in 2024.

Companies want people to remember them. They make their Super Bowl ads special. Some ads are really funny or weird. Some make people think.

Some of the biggest ads are for soda, snacks, and cars. Many people watch the Super Bowl just for the commercials.

Think About It

What makes an ad stand out to you?

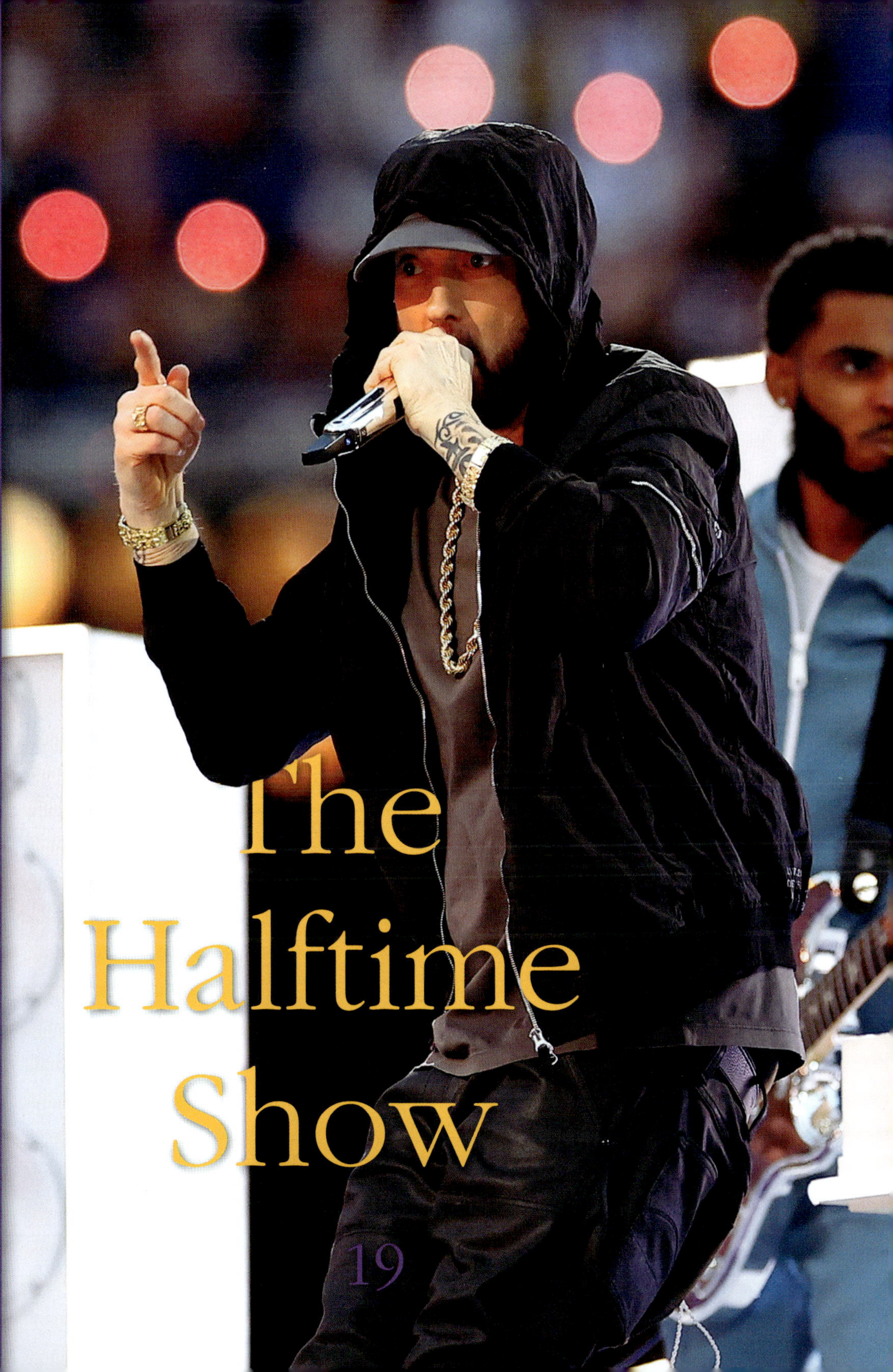

6

The Halftime Show

Halftime of a football game gives players a break. There is usually a show at halftime. A marching band might play. Dancers or a flag team might perform.

In 1993, the Super Bowl halftime show changed forever. Superstar Michael Jackson performed a short concert. After that, famous bands and singers have played at the Super Bowl every year.

Today's halftime shows are huge. Sets and stages are built on the field. There are light shows and special effects.

Did You Know?

A regular NFL halftime is 13 minutes long. The Super Bowl's halftime lasts about 30 minutes.

MORE TO EXPLORE

WHERE IN THE WORLD

SOFI STADIUM
2022 Super Bowl

ALLEGIANT STADIUM
2024 Super Bowl

STATE FARM STADIUM
2023 Super Bowl

MERCEDES-BENZ
STADIUM
2019 Super Bowl

RAYMOND JAMES
STADIUM
2021 Super Bowl

HARD ROCK STADIUM
2020 Super Bowl

FANTASTIC FACTS

The Super Bowl has been held in the Miami area 11 times. The city's Hard Rock Stadium has held the Super Bowl six times.

The 1972 Super Bowl was in New Orleans, Louisiana. It was the coldest of all time. The temperature was only 39 degrees Fahrenheit (3.9 degrees Celsius).

A ticket to the Super Bowl can cost between $6,000 and $60,000.

Twelve NFL teams have never won a Super Bowl. Four have never played in the big game at all.

The Super Bowl is named after a bouncy rubber ball called a Superball.

Only two teams have won the Super Bowl in their home stadium. The teams are the Los Angeles Rams and the Tampa Bay Buccaneers.

MORE TO EXPLORE

COOL COMPARISONS

Most Super Bowl Appearances
(as of 2024)

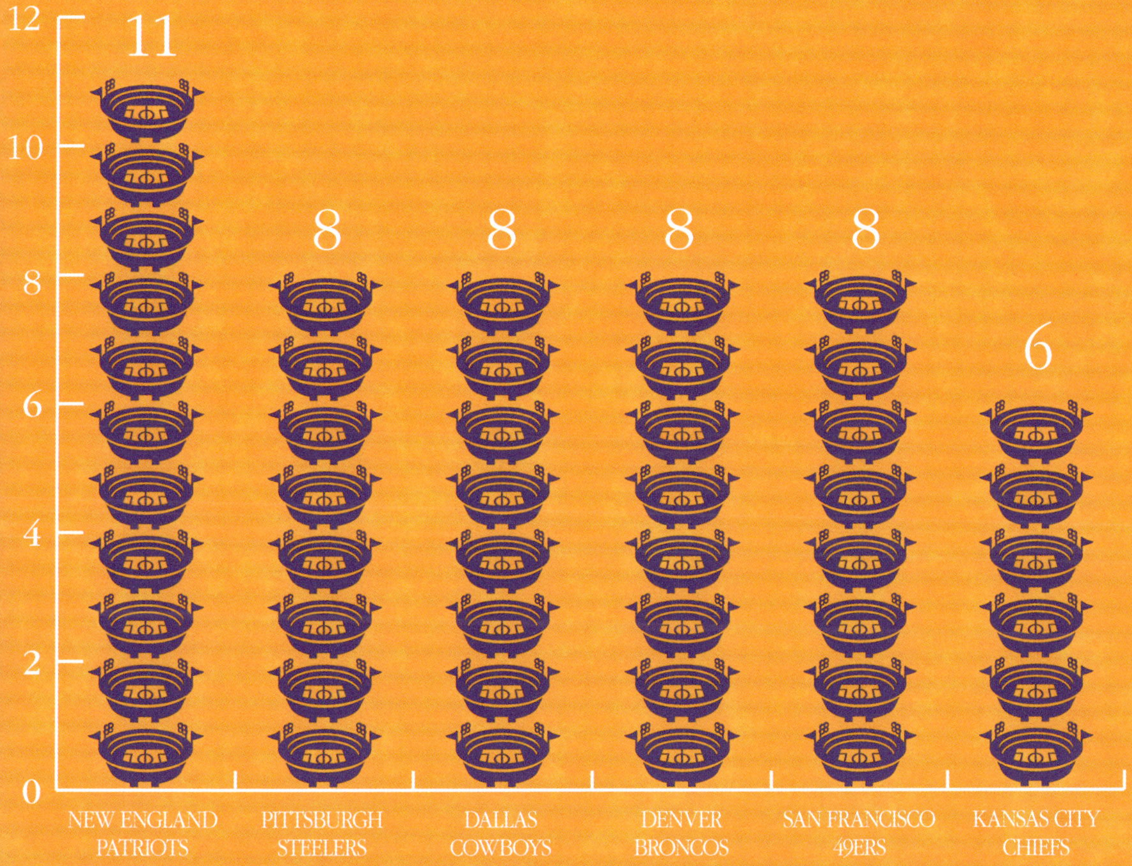

MORE TO EXPLORE

RESOURCES

Glossary

advertise (ADD-vur-tyz) To bring public attention to a product or service.

expert (EKS-purt) A person who knows a great deal about a specific topic.

halftime (HAFF-tym) A brief time of rest between two halves of a game.

kickoff (KIK-ahf) The kick that starts play in a game.

media (MEE-dee-uh) The radio stations, TV stations, and newspapers through which information is communicated to the public.

Super Bowl (SOO-pur BOHL) The championship game of the NFL.

Read More

Leed, Percy. *Football's Super Bowl.* Minneapolis: Lerner Publications, 2025.

Whiting, Jim. *New England Patriots.* Mankato: Creative Education/Creative Paperbacks, 2020.

Index

• Top Rank is an imprint of Black Rab Books. • Edited by Alissa Thielges • Designed by Danny Nanos • Photographs © Alamy: Xinhua, 7; Getty: Diamond Images, 14, Focus On Sp 6, Icon Sports Wire, 5, 8–9, 10–11, Issarawat Tattong, 7, Kevin C. Cox, 2–3, 19, Maddie Meyer, cover, 4–5, RJ Sangosti, 20, Robert Deutschm 15, Wally Skalij, 12–13; Newscom: Doug Murray/Icon Sportswire, cover; Shutterstock: Cincila, 18, Feng Cheng, 21, JeniFoto, 16, Katherine Wel 21, Kit Leong, 21, Leonard Zhukovsky, 21, M. Unal Ozmen, 18, Max Zafiro, 18, Nuttadol Kanperm, 16–17, SAHACHATZ, 18, The Image Engi 18, Vincent Doyle, 21 • Printed in the United States of America. **Library of Congress Cataloging-in-Publication Data:** Names: Silverman, Dr 1982- author. | Williams, Heather DiLorenzo, author. | Title: Great Super Bowl traditions / Drew Silverman & Heather Dilorenzo Williams. | Descripti Mankato, MN: Black Rabbit Books, [2025] | Series: Top rank. NFL at a glance | Ages 8–11 | Grades 4-6 | Identifiers: LCCN 2023052727 | IS 9781645822875 (library binding) | ISBN 9781645823193 (paperback) | ISBN 9781645823513 (ebook) | Subjects: LCSH: Super Bowl Juvenile literature. | Classification: LCC GV956.2.S8 S55 2025 | DDC 796.332/648—dc23/eng/20231116